JOHNNY

APPLESEED

THE STORY OF A LEGEND

JOHNNY

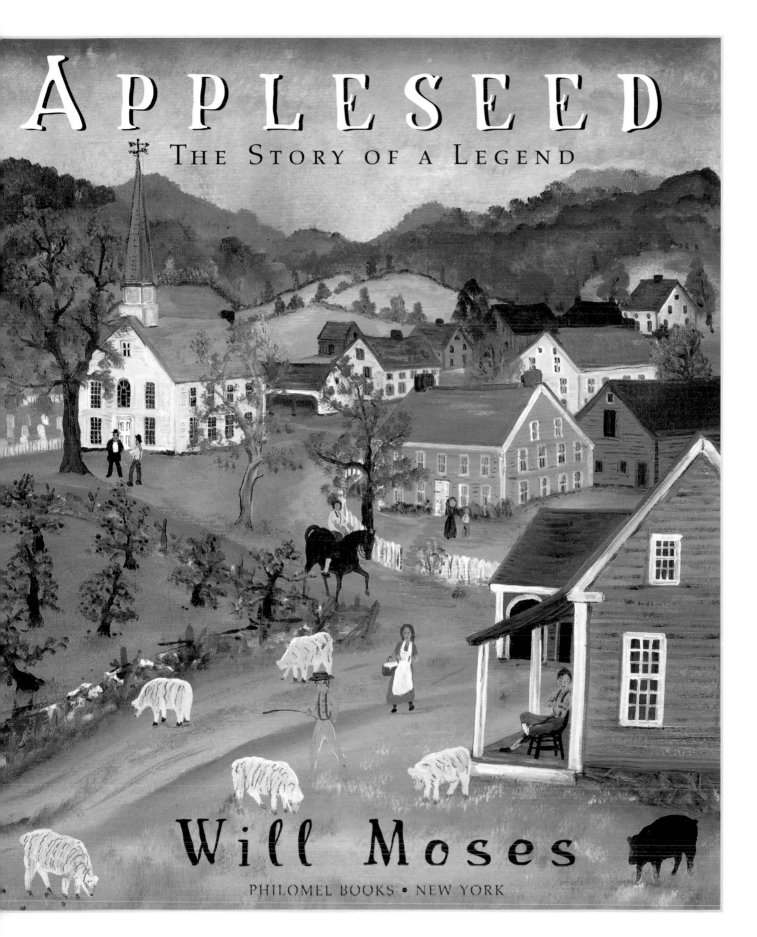

APPLESEED
THE STORY OF A LEGEND

Will Moses

PHILOMEL BOOKS • NEW YORK

PATRICIA LEE GAUCH, EDITOR

PHILOMEL BOOKS
a division of Penguin Putnam Books for Young Readers,
345 Hudson Street, New York, NY 10014.
Philomel Books, Reg. U.S. Pat. & Tm. Off. Published simultaneously in Canada.
Manufactured in China by South China Printing Co. Ltd.   The text is set in 14-point Goudy.
Library of Congress Cataloging-in-Publication Data
Moses, Will.   Johnny Appleseed : The story of a legend / Will Moses.   p. cm.
1. Appleseed, Johnny, 1774–1845—Juvenile literature. 2. Apple growers—United States—Biography—Juvenile literature.
3. Frontier and pioneer life—Middle West—Juvenile literature. [1. Appleseed, Johnny, 1774–1845. 2. Apple growers.
3. Frontier and pioneer life.] I. Title.   SB63.C46 M67 2001   634'.11'092—dc21   [B]   00-044600
ISBN 0-399-23153-6
3 5 7 9 10 8 6 4

For Good Old Clyde—A Great Friend

AUTHOR'S NOTE

Nearly everyone has heard a tale or two about Johnny Appleseed. Now, what many people may not realize is that Johnny Appleseed was, in fact, a real flesh-and-blood man who lived a truly amazing and exciting life two centuries ago. John Chapman, or as we more commonly know him, Johnny Appleseed, is one of the great characters from American history. He lived his life by a strict code of morality, honesty and kindness to all creatures. He devoted his life to helping others help themselves, providing apple trees, herbs and friendship to settlers all across the wild frontier of Middle America. John Chapman was a pioneer, probably this country's first nurseryman, certainly one of its great agriculturists and, without a doubt, a great man.

Johnny Appleseed lived simply in a very simple era. Few detailed accounts of individual lives were kept on the raw frontier, and much of what we know about Johnny has been pieced together over time from a variety of local historical sources. Weaving together the life of Johnny Appleseed from these sources has been great fun. There are few characters from our past that offer better fodder for colorful storytelling than this woodsman. Writing about—and illustrating—his life has been a wonderful opportunity.

In many ways, Johnny Appleseed represents the best qualities of the American character. He was born on the brink of the American Revolution and, as a young man, helped blaze the trail westward. His apple trees and orchards served as living beacons for settlers to follow on their migration. Today, it is Johnny's good character that may serve as an even better and stronger beacon to follow. He was genuinely good-natured, filled with kindness and humanity; had an industrious, independent spirit; and was a generous friend to all—traits we can still admire.

—W. M.

It was in 1774, September to be exact, when the apples were hanging heavy and red on the trees, that John Chapman was born in Leominster, Massachusetts, to Elizabeth and Nathaniel Chapman.

But to tell the truth, not too many noticed just then. The countryside was all abuzz with talk of revolution—with standing up to the British and their high taxes, which had begun to pinch folks too much and all too often.

In fact, John's own father was a Minuteman, a farmer or shopkeeper who would, on a minute's notice,

rush to defend the American colonies from attack. And in 1776, when John was only two years old, his father did indeed rush off to do battle with the British at Concord, Massachusetts.

Now, little Johnny Chapman didn't know anything about fighting and war. And, no doubt, he was even too young to remember his own mother dying the very year his father left for the war. But Johnny's grandma and grandpa took good care of him and his sister Elizabeth, looking after them for the next four years while their father was fighting. And then, just before Johnny's sixth birthday, Nathaniel Chapman sent word back home that he was going to marry a woman named Lucy and had found a little farm near Longmeadow, Massachusetts, to settle on.

So, Johnny and Elizabeth said good-bye to their grandparents and went to live with their pa and Lucy on the little farmstead in Longmeadow. And it was there, surrounded by lush meadows and inviting woods, not far from the banks of the Connecticut River, that Johnny and Elizabeth grew up. And it was there on that little farm that Johnny's father and new mother raised ten more children besides!

Growing up as he did probably shaped Johnny into the man he became. Well, you can just imagine—twelve children, all in one small farmhouse! And while Johnny liked children, with their singing and playing and scrapping, and though he'd join with all the other kids at school during the week and again on Sunday for church and Bible reading, it seems certain his most cherished moments were those he spent alone in the woods.

In fact, if you were ever to ask Johnny Chapman where his home was, like as not, he would look to the nearest forest and nod, *Over there*. Over where the autumn maples and oaks turned crimson, yellow and gold in the fall, and the glens were rich with the scent of earthy pine.

In those wild woods a young man like Johnny Chapman could live as he wanted, free like the Indians and the animals.

And so, when he was in his early twenties, no doubt with thoughts of living like the Indians and the animals in mind, Johnny picked up and left Longmeadow for good. He knew civilization was spreading like a brush fire, pushing the wild lands farther and farther away. But he was determined to go where the wild lands still were: west to the frontier.

Now, Johnny didn't exactly know where the frontier was or what he would do once he got there, but he figured all that would come to him naturally enough. Things like that always did.

Right from the start, Johnny Chapman traveled with the seasons, and that made good sense. He left Massachusetts late in the spring when the world was warm and green and lush and the apple trees were just shaking off their blossoms. And with little more than the clothes on his back, some cornmeal and hardtack in his pack and a few coins in his purse, Johnny set out.

Up and over the Berkshire and Taconic mountains, past meadows, Johnny clambered, till one day, he dropped down into the Hudson River valley. And maybe it was there that the seed of a great idea took root in Johnny's mind. Walking amongst those rich Dutch farms, he must have noticed how each one of those bountiful farms had an orchard, brimming full of apple trees. And just maybe, as he walked past an orchard, he plucked a little green apple from its

bough, thinking that he might have a use for an apple himself someday. For the present, though, he would let this idea rest. After all, he had to keep moving west with the seasons, looking for the frontier.

Mostly, Johnny walked, sometimes following the old Indian trails. Sometimes, when he could, he would hitch a ride in a canoe or bump along with a settler family who was heading his way. More and more, though, Johnny traveled like the Indians themselves, living right off the land, eating berries, nuts and roots. And when night fell, he slept in a hammock strung between branches or else he burrowed deep into a blanket of fallen leaves. No matter how rough it got, he loved sleeping out at night, watching that great night sky filled with its big yellow moon and twinkling stars.

But then along about October, the autumn winds from Canada began to blow down from the Great Lakes. Johnny put on another shirt and wound an old scarf around his head. And just as it was starting to get really cold, his shoes gave out. He stuffed them with mullein leaves and bound them with twine and rags. Food was becoming scarce, too!

Johnny never did stop and say, "I've finally found the frontier." No, in fact, you could say the frontier found him. That winter of 1797, when he came over the Allegheny plateau right at the top of Pennsylvania, a tremendous storm blew down on him. All Johnny could do was to take shelter in a big, hollow tree, curling up like a winter bear, waiting the storm out. When the sky finally cleared, there was three feet of fresh snow.

Johnny knew he could go no farther. So, with hunger and cold hard upon him and his strength failing, he made himself a pair of crude snowshoes from hemlock branches and vine, and trudged on to Warren, Pennsylvania. For many a year afterward, folks around Warren spoke of how the man who came to be known as Johnny Appleseed suddenly appeared one day. "Blew into town on a snow squall," they said.

Starving and nearly frozen to death, Johnny was lucky to be alive. And maybe it was while he was there in Warren, recovering from his scrape with death, that Johnny Appleseed had the vision. The one many a settler family claimed he spoke of, where shining angels visited Johnny in the night, revealing to him a vision of a shimmering, heavenly community surrounded by beautiful apple trees.

The angels told Johnny that it was his mission to wander about the country, planting apple trees as he went, "so that the wilderness might be glad and blossom forth with fruit."

There is no doubt that Johnny was a profoundly spiritual man, and there is no doubt that something deeply moved him that winter of 1797. Because, when

the warm spring weather came, Johnny sprang to action and quickly found a rich plot of land on the banks of the Brokenstraw River, about six miles from Warren.

There in the woods he built a little cabin, raising the walls one log at a time all by himself. (Although when the cabin was finished, there were plenty of nights when he didn't sleep a wink inside those walls—he had gotten used to sleeping under the stars, smelling the scent of the changing seasons, listening to the creaking of the tall trees and the soft rustle of the night creatures.)

In the early days on the Brokenstraw, Johnny didn't have many neighbors, but there were a few trading posts here and there. Now, the trouble with trading posts, as he quickly found out, was that in order to get what you want, you need to have something to trade!

Johnny managed to swap this for that and that for this and wound up with a flock of chickens for eggs, a few goats for milk and enough seeds for a garden. Loving honey as he did, Johnny made himself some bee skeps and attracted swarms of bees to them. Now he had honey to eat and some to trade.

But more importantly, from the cider mills around Warren, Johnny collected apple seeds by the bag- and bucketful, carefully planting each one in the fertile

soil near his cabin. And it was only a short while before he had little apple trees growing right there on the Brokenstraw. Johnny thought they looked a lot like the trees he had seen in his dreams!

Now he really had something to trade. Apples! Apples were good for just about everything, weren't they? They were good for cooking or preserving—you could make dried apples, apple butter, applesauce, apple pie, apple cider, apple brandy, applejack, apple vinegar and best of all, apples just tasted so good!

Pioneers knew how important apples were; even the written law said that every new homestead must plant fifty apple trees. An orchard showed a settler's intention to stay put and work the land. So, Johnny figured, apple trees were just what the frontier needed, and he'd supply them.

Now, just when people started calling Johnny "Johnny Appleseed" is hard to say. Settlers always said that Johnny would be among the first to call at their cabins. He would appear suddenly, walking out of the dark woods, his long hair and whiskers usually all a-tangle and his friendly, piercing black eyes peeping out from his weathered face. Oftentimes his feet were bare and he was always

dressed in old cast-off clothing, sometimes a long, old, tattered farmer's coat, but always perched on his head would be his trademark—an outlandish hat—a soup pot one day, a pasteboard cap the next. Strolling up to a cabin for the first time appearing as he did, with a few apple-tree seedlings clutched in his big callused hands, gifts for the settlers, Johnny was not someone people soon forgot!

Early on, though, despite his odd ways, people sensed the genuine goodness in Johnny. Even the Indians—the Seneca, Maumee, Wyandot. Although one day, they say, Johnny ran into a band of rampaging Indians who didn't know he was a friend and didn't give him a chance to tell! They chased him over the hills for a long ways before he managed to slip into a lake and hide himself among the reeds and cattails.

Even then, those Indians didn't give up, and poor Johnny had to lie there hidden, all quiet and still, for such a long time that he fell sound asleep! The Indians didn't catch Johnny that day. They didn't catch him the time he ran all along a good part of the Ohio frontier raising the alarm warning settlers that a band of unfriendly Indians was on the warpath, though they were hot on his heels!

Most of the time, though, Johnny and the Indians got along just fine—after all, they were a lot alike.

Even the animals seemed to know what a good man Johnny Appleseed was. Johnny always thought animals were some of God's most special creatures, and animals seemed to understand that. Folks said that he cared for creatures a lot of people would just as soon forget! Why, one day he was mowing the grass in his orchard when he disturbed a big old rattlesnake. The snake, as quick as lightning, rose up and bit Johnny hard. Without thinking,  Johnny swung his scythe and cut that snake in half. They say Johnny nearly came to tears, he was so upset about what he had done to the poor old scaly snake.

And when it came to bees, Johnny was most respectful. No beehive was ever too high for Johnny Appleseed to inspect. He would clamber up even the most forbidding bee trees just to say hello to the bees and sample a little of their delicious honey. He would only sample, though, and never take it all! Didn't the bees need food for winter, too?

Soon, stories began to pop up all across the frontier about the odd, kindly man who lived alone in the woods growing his apple trees. And it's awfully hard to know which stories are true, but his neighbors swore, if there was ever a broken-down horse or mule left to wander the woods, Johnny would be sure to take it in, fatten it and nurse it back to good health. And when those old animals were spruced up again, they'd either have a job helping Johnny or Johnny'd find them a good home.

Some folks said that Johnny Appleseed could even talk to the animals. That even wolves would converse with him. And it just may be true, because one of

the favorite stories was how one day he found a young wolf, cruelly caught in a trap, near the banks of the Brokenstraw River. Johnny just spoke kindly to the animal and gently set him free without so much as a scratch. They say that for years after, that same wolf followed Johnny at a distance, watching over him, making sure that no harm ever came his way.

Others say that Johnny Appleseed never killed an animal (except for that old snake) at all, and that probably is not true. A man in the wilderness had to take enough to survive. But taking animals was probably never Johnny Appleseed's first choice. He preferred to live in harmony with the wild creatures, which may be why there are so many stories about Johnny and animals. And who knows which ones are true? That hunter's story, the one about finding Johnny Appleseed in the woods playing with black bear cubs while the mother bear looked on, well, it might be true.

And so might the tale of Johnny crawling into a big hollow log, trying to get

out of some blizzardy weather. When he found a mother bear and her cubs already curled up inside, he declared, "Why, you poor things, I'll not turn you out of your own house on a night such as this!" And with that, he crawled back out of the log and slept under the hemlocks, in the cold, snowy air, for the rest of that long night.

Johnny Appleseed was a strange fellow, no question, but he was also enterprising. Before long, his orchards and nurseries checkered the banks of the Brokenstraw and nearby French Creek. But even though Johnny was enterprising, he wasn't much of a businessman. If a family was so poor they couldn't afford to buy his trees, he gave them apple seedlings anyway. Money just wasn't that important to him. Being good to a fellow creature—even the human kind—was.

Before too many years had gone by, civilization caught up to Johnny again. And as is sure to happen when too many people start living too close to one another, there was some dispute over the ownership of the land Johnny had settled on. Johnny decided the best thing to do was to move on.

He could see that the frontier had passed him by anyway, and it was time for him to catch up to it again. In the Ohio Territory, there would be plenty of land for him!

But Johnny's apple trees were all around him—the meadows and riverbanks along the Brokenstraw teemed with apple blossoms every spring—and moving west meant leaving his apple trees behind.

Then a great idea struck Johnny Appleseed—nobody knows just how or when, but it certainly did. He would go to the cider mills and collect all the seeds he could carry, and then he would dig up his best seedlings and take the seeds and seedlings west with him! Once he found the frontier, he would find new spots to plant his trees and start his nurseries all over again.

It was a spring day early in the 1800s when someone first spotted Johnny Appleseed dropping down the Ohio River, paddling two Indian canoes lashed together, each brimming with leather sacks filled with apple seeds and bundles of sprouting apple-tree seedlings. Down the river he floated, all the way to Marietta, where he entered the Muskingum River and proceeded to make his way up the Walhonding and Black Fork rivers.

As Johnny went along, he would stop at every inviting spot he found and plant his seeds, once again telling everyone he saw that what they needed were apples! You could do about any darn thing you wanted with them. Eat them fresh or put them away for winter. You could dry apples or press them, or even make applejack. And there was nothing better than apple butter on corn bread. Why, apples would keep you alive on the frontier!

It was that mission again, sharing his apple trees with as many settlers as he possibly could. One thing was certain: If all the western frontier was abloom with apple trees—from north to south and east to west—that would be fine with him.

Back in those Ohio days, you might have seen Johnny Appleseed yourself, canoeing the Muskingum or Ohio rivers, taking his seedlings here or there. You might have seen his lanky frame coming down the trail, dressed in one of those outlandish costumes, his long black hair blowing in the breeze, piercing dark eyes taking in everything, leading an old pack horse toting seeds.

Or you might have spied him planting his seedlings, bent over in the sunshine, preparing the ground to receive the promising little trees, gently rooting each slender shoot into the rich earth.

And then after a few years, you would have seen the once fallow meadows along those Ohio rivers—the Muskingum, the Walhonding, the Licking Creek, all the way up to the headwaters of the Black Fork—spring alive with Johnny's trees, blossoming pink, green and white.

Now, the funny thing about Johnny Appleseed was that the tales about him grew almost as fast as his apple trees. That's not really so remarkable when you think about it. After all, a life on the frontier was a hard one. A settler family had to build a life for themselves out of nothing but their strong backs, their quick wits and the land they settled.

There were worries aplenty, all right; keeping warm through winters when the snow was up to the cabin windows, staving off Indian attacks and fending away hungry wolves were just everyday problems!

So it wasn't surprising that when pioneer families gathered around the fire at night, they told stories, oftentimes tall stories! Johnny, well, he was one fine storyteller, and they say his stories were taller than just about any. So folks just naturally swapped and traded Johnny Appleseed yarns from cabin to cabin. And with each telling, those stories seemed to grow a little bit more.

It was probably during those early years in Ohio that the legend of Johnny Appleseed took root. There were all the

stories about his encounters with bears and Indians, but new ones were being told, too! Folks loved the one about Johnny riding the ice floe.

Seems Johnny was paddling downriver in early spring, just as the ice broke up. Suddenly he found himself among some really big ice and it got to crowding his canoe, bumping him so that he feared he might tip over and drown! Only one thing to do. Johnny jumped out and hauled his canoe up onto a big ice cake and merrily floated along the rest of the way, waving and tipping his cap to folks on the bank as he went.

And there were the hero stories, like the ones about Johnny surviving by walking in snow—barefoot. Or how he'd step out of a forest to help a traveler, maybe to warn them about Indians, or to restore a lost child. Then, having saved the day, the mysterious Johnny would disappear back into the dark woods!

Almost all of the stories folks swapped about Johnny told of what a kind and generous man he was. One man told of the time he met Johnny Appleseed on the trail and Johnny was shin deep in cold mud, wearing no shoes. The man kindly gave Johnny an old pair of boots from his own pack. But the next day, back in town, the traveling man saw Johnny again and he was once again barefoot.

"What in the world did you do with the boots I gave you yesterday?" he inquired of Johnny.

"Well, sir, I came upon a poor soul who needed them worse than I," was his only reply.

Johnny Appleseed was an avid reader, and he believed others should learn to read, too. But there were no libraries out there in the woods, so he gladly shared his own books with frontier families, oftentimes ripping chapters out so that each family could read a bit and then pass it along to their neighbor.

If Johnny happened to share a meal with you, folks said, it would be his custom after the meal to stand before the hearth and inquire of the family gathered about him, "Would you like to hear some news right fresh from heaven?" Whereupon he would produce his tattered Bible and commence telling old Bible stories, his voice rising and falling, strong and thrilling, till the Spirit was upon everyone.

Tall tales or not, a few things are pretty certain. Johnny Appleseed lived for the settlers and the animals around him, always helping whenever he could. And Johnny lived for his apple trees, making sure each orchard was tended to properly so that when folks needed apples, they were ready.

It is pretty certain, too, that Johnny didn't live as much for himself as maybe he should have. As he grew older, his hair got wilder and wilder and his clothes became even more of a shambles, sometimes nothing more than a sack covering his bony frame. Of course, he kept giving his shoes away, and the only thing that kept the sun from Johnny's eyes and the rain from his head was one of his crazy hats.

So, sometime around 1830, Johnny's half-sister Persis, who had come west with her family, convinced Johnny to come and live with her in the village of Perrysville, Ohio. Johnny would be welcome to live there with Persis, her husband—and their thirteen children!

Well, it was a house full of children all over again, just as it had been all those years ago in Longmeadow. But believe it or not, that is probably what Johnny Appleseed said yes to. Maybe he'd come to be just a mite bit lonely, living alone in the woods all this time!

Anyway, he packed his few goods up in a bundle and said good-bye to the wilderness. Said good-bye to sleeping out under the stars on warm nights. Said good-bye to the animals that wandered friendly around his cabin, and went to the village to live.

For the next few years, he went to supper like ordinary folk. And here, with his relatives around him, he spent the evenings in the glow of the firelight, reading his Bible or spinning tales, thrilling his nieces and nephews with each new adventure.

Johnny helped out around the farmstead and still tended to his seedlings and trees. And he spent a lot of time with the boys and girls of Perrysville, devoting whole afternoons to playing with them, buying them treats and giving out hair ribbons to the girls. Clearly, Johnny adored children—maybe it was for their simplicity and goodness.

Probably it was a surprise to some that he grew so comfortable in Perrysville. Some folks even claimed that when he moved in with Persis, he slept in a bed with sheets and a quilt pretty regularly.

The fact was, by this time, Johnny had apple trees growing from western Pennsylvania to the middle of Ohio. They had been there when the people needed them, just the way he had seen it in his vision long ago. Besides his own nurseries, an awful lot of settlers—too many to count—had their own orchards, thanks to Johnny Appleseed.

Maybe Johnny began to wonder if his job was done. He'd forget the frontier, settle down right there in Perrysville and be part of a family for good. Some town folk even gossiped that maybe Johnny was falling in love with comely Nancy Tannehill!

Then one day, as some legends have it, Johnny was on the trail west of Mansfield, Ohio, when he met a strapping boy named David Hunter. They shared a lunch of corn cakes there on a trailside log, and David told Johnny his pitiful tale.

Turns out that poor David's mother and father had died, leaving him to raise his nine brothers and sisters, and he was only seventeen years old! How was he managing it, Johnny wanted to know—the seeds of an idea already growing in his brain. Not very well, the boy replied.

"Well," Johnny wondered, "why don't you get yourself some apple trees?"

"Apple trees?"

"Yes, apple trees."

Johnny knew that David had no money to buy apple trees and when David said so, Johnny told him he wanted to give him the trees. So, a few days later, David Hunter took fifty or sixty small trees from Johnny, and he and his nine brothers and sisters planted them on the land their mother and father had homesteaded. Most likely Johnny helped, too; he always liked to make sure his trees were planted right.

Maybe it was a fall day when the woodland colors along the edge of the field were turning crimson and yellow, or it might have been in the springtime, when the forest was budding pink and green. Whenever it was, spring or fall, David Hunter and his brothers and sisters, and maybe even Johnny Appleseed himself, planted those apple trees. And before long an orchard full of strong, bountiful trees covered a hillside on the Hunter farm.

Perhaps it was seeing that people still needed him—or maybe Johnny had just grown weary of town life, whatever the reason, Johnny decided that it was time to head west again.

It wasn't easy for him to leave his sister and her family, especially those thirteen nieces and nephews. All those tear-streaked faces bidding their old uncle good-bye. No, it wasn't easy, but just the same, he picked up his belongings and went.

Just as before, he took his seedlings with him, loading all he could on some of his faithful old animals. After a time, traveling with the seasons as always, he made it to Fort Wayne, Indiana. Now, Fort Wayne was closer to the frontier, just the way he liked it! And once again, he got himself a canoe, loaded it with seeds and seedlings and floated out onto the rivers around northern Indiana, rivers like the Maumee, the Elkhart, the St. Marys and the St. Joseph (some say, all the way up to Michigan!).

His story was the same, and he told it to anyone who would listen: What you need are apples. Why, you can eat them off the tree—you can cook with them or dry them, make apple butter and apple cider and apple vinegar . . .

Johnny planted, sold and traded apple trees all across the Indiana frontier, visiting new cabins, making new friends and sleeping out under the stars. Fact is, he never really left the wilderness again. And just like in the old days, he traveled with the seasons, making his way down the streams and over the old Indian trails, checking his trees, moving some, planting some and pruning others. It was his way of life!

But Johnny Appleseed was no longer a young man. True, he was still surprising some people with his spunk—there was the story of how, at age sixty-eight, Johnny was helping out at a house-raising when he spied a barn fire way down in the valley. He sounded out the alarm and then outran all the younger men and boys, only to reach the fire first and have no one to help him put it out.

But some folks began to consider Johnny to be a bit strange with his wild hair

and tattered garb, mainly those who didn't really know him or hadn't heard all the tales of his younger days. They definitely hung back when Johnny happened around, though none of this would have mattered at all to Johnny; it was his mission that counted!

So it is good to know that Johnny died the way he would have wanted— taking care of his trees.

Word came to Johnny one cold, wet spring morning that there was trouble at one of his best orchards on the St. Joseph River. Wandering cattle had broken down the orchard fence and were rooting throughout the orchard, eating buds, bark and trees!

Old Johnny started off at a dash, hair flying and coattails flapping in the cool, damp morning air. Time was important. He didn't stop for water and he didn't stop to take a rest, like he should have. No, Johnny kept on going, the cold wind and rain seeping in around the seams of his coat. As fast as he could go, Johnny made his way over the Indian trails and through muddy fields. Finally, he came to the little road that led past his orchard.

When poor Johnny arrived, the trees of his orchard were March bare. Nary a leaf nor bud was showing, unless you looked real close. And there, smack dab in the middle of that orchard, were the cows, happily chewing away at his trees.

Johnny, puffing hard after his long hike, thundered in amongst the big beasts hooting and shooing, pushing each animal, bony bottom by bony bottom, back through the fence and out of the orchard.

Not surprisingly, by the time those cows were finally evicted, old Johnny was tuckered out. Weary as he was, though, he knew he had to fix up that rotten fence or those darn cows would be right back in. Cold, worn to the bone and with night falling, Johnny made his way to the home of a friend, William Worth, where he ate supper and even led a rousing prayer service one last time.

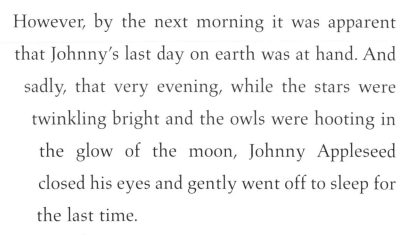

However, by the next morning it was apparent that Johnny's last day on earth was at hand. And sadly, that very evening, while the stars were twinkling bright and the owls were hooting in the glow of the moon, Johnny Appleseed closed his eyes and gently went off to sleep for the last time.

Johnny Appleseed had planted tens of thousands of apple trees by the time he died that spring of 1845. Throughout his life, he always tried to do right by his fellow man, by the animals and by the earth. He was a godly man, a simple man and a great American character, loved and respected by all who knew him.

He wouldn't have wanted a fuss made over him, but the tales of his good deeds and adventures are so many and so great that "Johnny Appleseed stories" are still being told around the campfire. And they always will be told, as long as there is goodness in our hearts and apple trees still blossom in the spring.

ACKNOWLEDGMENTS

I think I have Johnny's story about right but not without some help. I would like to thank Patti Gauch, my editor, for her good ideas, sound judgment and encouragement, and Alison Keehn for her research assistance. I would also like to thank historian Paul J. Benoit, who helped verify some of the factual details about John Chapman's life. The Longmeadow Historical Society, the Leominster Historical Society and the Bellville Historical Society were all of great help in the research for this book.

If there are kudos for this work, I willingly share the praise. If there is criticism, I bear that burden solely.

Will Moses

BIBLIOGRAPHY

Greene, Carol. *John Chapman: The Man Who Was Johnny Appleseed.* Chicago: Children's Press, 1991.

Haley, W. D. "Johnny Appleseed—A Pioneer Hero." *Harper's New Monthly Magazine* 43, no. 258 (1871): 830–836.

Price, Robert. *Johnny Appleseed: Man and Myth.* Bloomington: Indiana University Press, 1954.

Rodger, Linda M., and Mary S. Rogeness, eds. *Reflections of Longmeadow, 1783/1983.* Canaan, N.H.: Published for the Longmeadow Historical Society by Phoenix Pub., 1983.